Sailor Cats

Sailor Cats

BY EMILY WHITTLE

ILLUSTRATED BY JERI BURDICK

GREEN TIGER PRESS

Published by Simon & Schuster

New York   London   Toronto   Sydney   Tokyo   Singapore

GREEN TIGER PRESS
Simon & Schuster Building, Rockefeller Center
1230 Avenue of the Americas, New York, New York 10020
Text copyright © 1993 by Emily Whittle
Illustrations copyright © 1993 by Jeri Burdick
All rights reserved including the right of reproduction
in whole or in part in any form.
GREEN TIGER PRESS is an imprint of Simon & Schuster.
Designed by Sylvia Frezzolini
Manufactured in the United States of America.

10 9 8 7 6 5 4 3 2 1

Library of Congress Cataloging-in-Publication Data
Whittle, Emily.   Sailor cats / by Emily Whittle;
illustrated by Jeri Burdick. p.   cm.
Summary: Bored with the summer heat, two cats sail out
to sea to learn what it is like to be sailors.
[1. Cats—Fiction. 2. Sailing—Fiction.] I. Burdick, Jeri, ill. II. Title.
PZ7.W61884Sai 1993   92-23418
[E]—dc20   CIP
                        AC
ISBN: 0-671-79933-9

To Iris and Miss Kitty,
Beijing and the memory of Sophie
who still floats under the stars.
                    —E.W. and J.B.

Ping

and Pong

were bored with the summer heat

and sailed out to sea
on a rubber tire
to learn what it was like
to be sailor cats.

To the sea,
the old tire weighed no more
than the shadow of clouds.
Ping and Pong
floated onto the great ocean
as happy as two cats
beside a goldfish pond.
But soon,
the sea did
what the sea does.
Calm ripples
swelled to towering waves.

Hours passed.
Fish after fish
slipped through their clumsy paws.
Their empty bellies
growled with hunger.
Under the hot sun,
they had only the sea
and their own salt tears
to drink.
They panted with thirst,
their pink tongues
hanging from their mouths
like wilted flowers.

All day,
Ping and Pong
held their wet tails high,
hugging the black tire
like frightened kittens
clinging to their mother's fur.
Dreams of glorious adventure
sank
into the dark waves
as unnoticed as forgotten toys.
Sharks,
who can smell fear,
quickly gathered around.

Darkness fell.

Under the full moon,
the two sailor cats
meowed and moaned
until they lost their voices.
They bobbed and drifted
through the black night
on the black sea
on the black tire—
their wide eyes
glowing like pearls.

When dawn arrived,
some leaping dolphins
spied them.

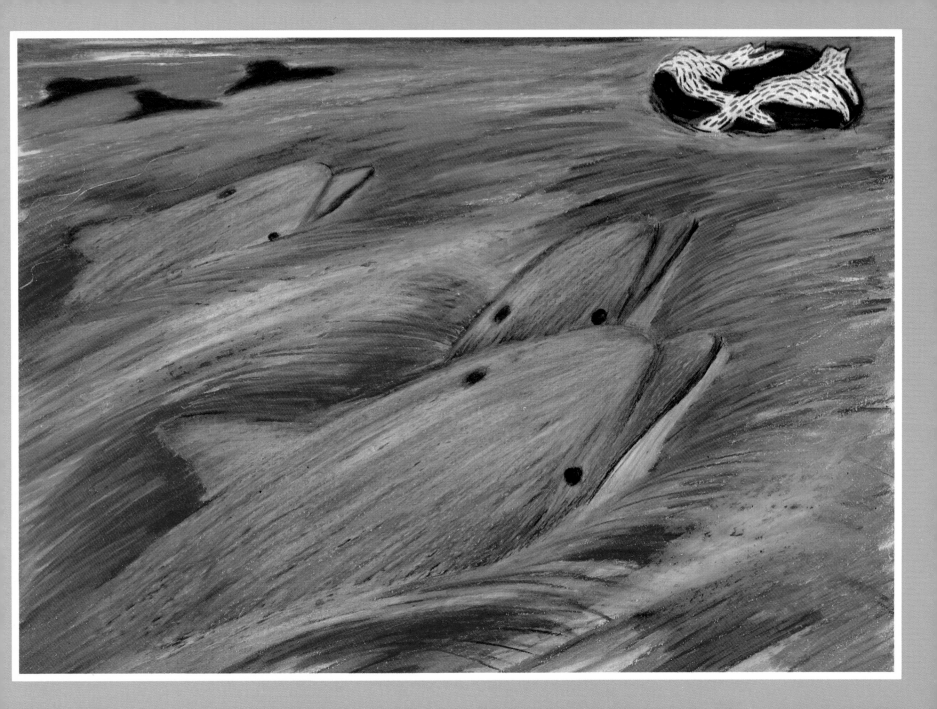

"These are not fish!"
the indignant dolphins cried.
And they pushed them
out of their waters
onto the dry land.

Scarcely breathing,
Ping and Pong
lay
as motionless
as broken shells.
"Are we dreaming?"
they wondered.
Neither the sea nor the sky
answered.
Finally, Ping and Pong
tested their trembling legs.
With happy purrs,
they shook the sea,
sand and fear
from their wet fur
and stood
on the firm ground
where cats belong.

Safe at home,
brave again,
(and just a little bit wise),

they will never forget
their night at sea
sailing under the open skies.

EMILY WHITTLE

is the author of Green Tiger's popular *The Fisherman's Tale,* also illustrated by Jeri Burdick. Artist, writer, bookbinder and jewelry designer, Ms. Whittle makes her home in Red Springs, North Carolina with her husband, sociology professor John Bowman.

JERI BURDICK

is a multitalented artist whose work is included in a number of museum collections, and has been exhibited in galleries throughout the U.S. and Canada. She is the illustrator of Green Tiger's *The Fisherman's Tale,* and lives in Eutawville, South Carolina.